D0537190

for Charlie.

I Wish I Could Count to a Million

Joyce Dunbar

Illustrated by Carol Thompson

Hodder
Children's
Books

A division of Hodder Headline Limited

British Library Cataloguing in Publication Data
A catalogue record of this book is available from the British Library.

ISBN 0340 79676 6 (HB)
ISBN 0340 79677 4 (PB)
10 9 8 7 6 5 4 3 2 1

Text copyright © Joyce Dunbar 1992
Illustrations copyright © Carol Thompson 1992

First published in 1992 by Simon and Schuster Young Books

This edition published in 2000 by Hodder Children's Books
a division of Hodder Headline Limited
338 Euston Road London NW1 3BH

The right of Joyce Dunbar to be identified as the author of this Work and the right
of Carol Thompson to be identified as the illustrator of this Work has been asserted
by them in accordance with the Copyright, Designs and Patents Act 1988.

Printed in Hong Kong

I wish I could . . .

fly like a bird,

swim like a tadpole.

But I CAN'T!

What I CAN do is . . .

hop,

skip,

and jump.

I wish I could . . .
ride my brother's
two-wheel bike,

skateboard,

walk on stilts.

But I CAN'T!

But I CAN scoot my tractor round the garden.

I wish I could . . .
climb trees like my cat,

see into the
bathroom
mirror,

reach the
biscuit tin.

But I CAN'T!

But I CAN slide down the slide at the park.

I wish I could . . .
whistle a tune,

spin a web like a spider,

catch a
tooth fairy.

But I CAN'T!

But I CAN blow big,
shiny bubbles.

I wish I could . . .
count to a million,

write in
straight lines,

read scary comics.

But I CAN'T!

But I CAN paint a lovely
funny picture . . .

cut out paper-chain people . . .

turn a head-
over-heels . . .

get dressed
all by myself.

So you see . . .

there are lots of things I CAN DO!